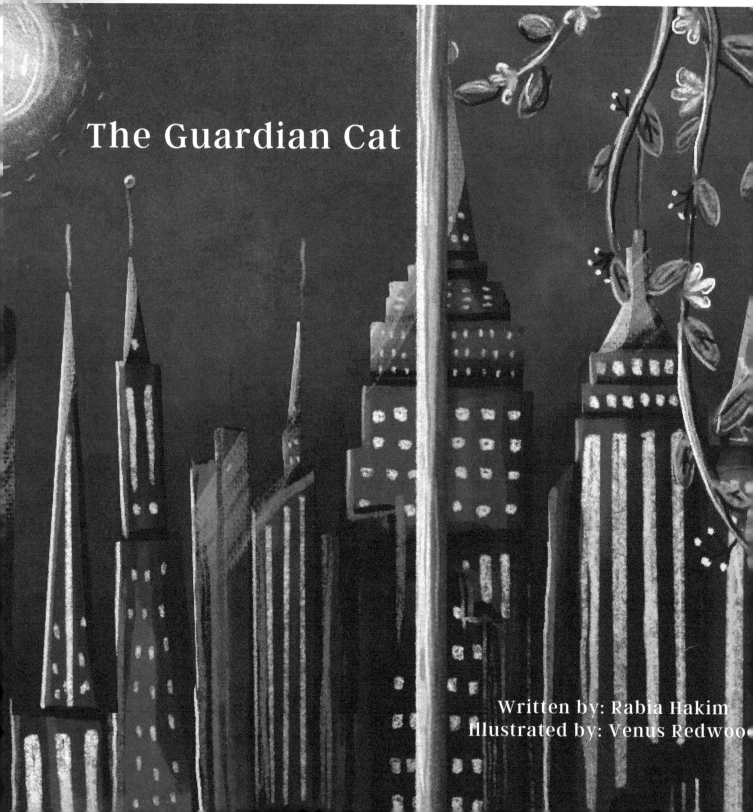

The Guardian Cat

Written by: Rabia Hakim
Illustrated by: Venus Redwood

Dedicated to my little nuggets,

Cat has guarded plants for many years.
He stands his post without any fears.

One day a baby appeared in Cat's lair.
With his big brown eyes, all he did was stare.

Cat was now tasked with his greatest challenge yet. To protect and guard the baby against every threat.

His first foe was the relentlessly annoying fly.
It buzzed around the baby and made him cry.

Cat heroically started to swat left and right.
Until the fly was finally out of sight.

On the night that water threatened
to submerge the baby,

Cat didn't hesitate,
or think maybe.

Cat quickly unrolled the toilet paper
and swirled it all around.

He saved the baby,
without making a sound.

When the baby was chased
by the rogue robot,

Cat gallantly tamed it,
without a second thought.

Cat vigilantly patrolled day and night.
But one day, his nemesis came into sight.

From underneath the couch,
Cat pounced quickly.

But the wicked red dot,
darted away swiftly.

Cat frantically tried to trap it in a cup.
The red dot escaped, leaving a mess to clean up.

Cat gathered all his strength,
and jumped a great length.

In the blinds, he got stuck,
while the red dot ran amuck.

Still, Cat's motivation did not fade,
but the baby knew it was time to aid.

The baby began to push the box with his hands,
to help cushion Cat's fall as he lands.

The baby rescued Cat,
and safely in the box they sat.

Cat and baby gaurded each other every night,
and the red dot never came back into sight.